This book belongs to

_____

Snow White

BY

The Brothers Grimm

Retold by Jennifer Greenway

ILLUSTRATED BY

Erin Augenstine

ARIEL BOOKS

ANDREWS AND McMEEL

KANSAS CITY

Library of Congress Cataloging-in-Publication Data

Greenway, Jennifer.
    Snow White / the Brothers Grimm ; retold by Jennifer Greenway ;
illustrated by Erin Augenstine.
        p.   cm.
    Summary: Retells the tale of the beautiful princess and her adventures
with the seven dwarfs she finds living in the forest.
    ISBN 0–8362–4906–2 (hard) : $6.95
    [1. Fairy tales. 2. Folklore—Germany.] I. Grimm, Jacob, 1785–1863.
II. Augenstine, Erin, ill. III. Schneewittchen. IV. Title.
PZ8.G84Sn   1991
398.22′0943—dc20   91–12134
                                                              CIP
                                                               AC

Design: Susan Hood and Mike Hortens
Art Direction: Armand Eisen, Mike Hortens, and Julie Phillips
Art Production: Lynn Wine
Production: Julie Miller and Lisa Shadid

Snow White

$\mathcal{O}$ne snowy winter day, a queen sat at the window sewing on a frame made of ebony. She pricked her finger with the needle, and three drops of blood fell in the snow on the windowsill.

The red blood looked so beautiful against the white snow that the queen exclaimed, "I wish I had a daughter as white as snow, red as blood, and black as ebony."

A short time later the queen gave birth to a daughter whose skin was as white as snow, whose cheeks were as red as blood, and whose hair was black as ebony. She named her child Snow White and not long after, the queen died.

Snow White grew up to be the most beautiful girl in the world. She was so good and kind that everyone who met her could not help but love her. Even the birds in the trees and the animals of the woods adored her.

When Snow White was still a child, her father took a second wife. She was a very beautiful woman, but proud and spiteful. She could not bear the thought that anyone else might be as beautiful as she.

Now this queen had a magic mirror and whenever she looked into it, she would say:

Mirror, mirror, on the wall,
Who's the fairest of them all?

And the mirror would reply:

You are the fairest of them all.

Each year, however, Snow White grew more beautiful. One day, when the queen looked into her mirror and asked it who was the fairest of them all, the mirror replied:

You are very fair, 'tis true.
But Snow White is more fair than you!

When the queen heard that she turned green with envy.

The queen called her huntsman before her. "You are to take Snow White into the forest," she said. "Kill her there, for I do not wish to set eyes on her again. And bring me the girl's heart in this box as proof that you have done as I have ordered."

The huntsman then led Snow White deep into the forest. But as he was drawing his hunting knife to kill her, Snow White cried, "Please spare my life! Let me run away into the forest and I will never come home again!"

Snow White was so young that the hunts-man took pity on her. He said to her, "Run into the woods, dear child!" Then he killed a deer and took its heart to the wicked queen as proof that Snow White was dead.

After he had gone, Snow White was alone in the forest. She was so frightened by the shapes of the trees and the rustling of the leaves that she began to run. Wild beasts sprang at her, but they did her no harm.

On she ran, over rocks and through brambles, until it began to grow dark. Snow White was so tired, she thought she could not take another step. Then up ahead she saw a tiny cottage.

Snow White went inside. Everything in the cottage was very clean and tidy—and also very small. There was a little table covered with a white cloth and set with seven little plates, each with a spoon and a knife and a cup. And against the wall, all in a row, were seven little beds.

Snow White was very hungry and thirsty. So she ate a bite of bread from each plate and drank a drop of water from each cup, for she did not want to take everything from any single one.

Then, as she was very tired, she lay down on one of the beds. Soon she was fast asleep.

A short while later, the owners of the cottage came home. They were seven dwarfs who spent their days mining in the mountains. As soon as they lit their candles the dwarfs saw that someone had been there while they were out.

"Who has been eating from my plate?" said the first.

"Who has been drinking from my cup?" cried the second.

And on it went, until the seventh dwarf caught sight of Snow White fast asleep in his bed. He called the others over, and they all stood and stared in wonder at the sleeping child.

"How beautiful she is!" they whispered, and they decided to let her go on sleeping.

The next morning, Snow White was frightened when she woke up and saw the seven dwarfs. But they smiled kindly at her and asked her her name.

"Snow White," she replied. Then she told them how her wicked stepmother had ordered the huntsman to kill her and how he had spared her her life.

"Why don't you stay here with us?" the dwarfs said. "You can cook and keep house for us, and we will take good care of you."

Snow White agreed, and so she kept the cottage for them and always had supper ready when they came home from working in the mountains.

As Snow White was alone all day, the dwarfs warned her to be careful.

"Do not let anyone in," they said, "for your wicked stepmother will surely discover where you are and come looking for you."

At that very moment the wicked queen looked into her magic mirror and asked:

Mirror, mirror, on the wall,
Who's the fairest one of all?

And the mirror replied:

You are very fair, 'tis true.
But in a cottage far away,
Where the seven dwarfs do stay,
Snow White is fairer still than you!

The wicked queen shook with rage. Snow White lived. Her magic mirror never lied. All day she schemed, until at last she settled on a plan to get rid of Snow White.

First the wicked queen made a poisoned apple. Half of it was snow-white and the other half was rosy red, and it looked delicious.

When the apple was ready, the queen disguised herself as a poor farm woman. Then she traveled to the seven dwarfs' cottage.

When the queen knocked on the door, Snow White came to the window.

"I cannot let anyone in," Snow White called out.

"But I only wish to sell you some of my apples," replied the farm woman. "Here, try one!" And she held out the poisoned apple.

But Snow White said, "No. I dare not!"

"Are you afraid I might poison you?" laughed the farm woman. "Look, I will cut the apple in two. You take the rosy red half, and I'll take the white." But Snow White did not know that the red half was poisoned.

"Very well," Snow White said, for the apple looked so delicious, she could not help herself. Eagerly, she bit into it. No sooner had she done so, than she fell down dead.

When the seven dwarfs came home that night they found Snow White lying pale and still on the ground. They called her name and tried to shake her awake, but it was no use. Snow White was truly dead.

At the palace, the wicked queen gazed into her magic mirror and asked who was the fairest of them all. The mirror replied:

You are the fairest of them all.

Finally, the wicked queen was satisfied.

The seven dwarfs wept over Snow White for three days. Then, it was time to bury her. But she looked as if she were still alive, and they could not bear to put her in the cold ground. So they made her a glass coffin and wrote her name on it in gold letters. Then they set it in the forest.

For a long time, Snow White lay in the glass coffin. Yet her beauty did not fade. One day a prince rode into the forest and saw the coffin. Snow White looked so lovely that he fell in love with her.

The prince begged the dwarfs to let him have Snow White's coffin. At last, they took pity on him and agreed.

The prince ordered his servants to carry Snow White in her glass coffin to his palace. But on the way, one of them tripped. The coffin fell, and the piece of poisoned apple flew from Snow White's throat.

Snow White opened her eyes. "Where am I?" she cried, looking up at the prince.

"You are with me," he replied, "and I wish you to marry me and stay with me forever."

The prince looked so kind and sincere that Snow White said, "Yes." And their wedding was celebrated with great joy. The seven dwarfs all came and danced and cheered.

As for the wicked queen, she was so angry that she ran into the forest and was never seen again. And with no one to wish them harm, Snow White and the prince lived happily ever after.